D0122801

The
Thanksgiving
Beast Feast

KAREN GRAY RUELLE

Holiday House / New York

For Deb,
Sally, and Susan:
Treasured friends and
fellow feast-beasts!

Reading Level: 1.9

Library of Congress Cataloging-in-Publication Data
Ruelle, Karen Gray.
The Thanksgiving beast feast / by Karen Gray Ruelle.--1st ed.
p. cm.
"1.9"
Summary: Harry and his sister, Emily, celebrate Thanksgiving by making a
holiday feast for the animals in their yard.
ISBN 0-8234-1511-2
[1. Thanksgiving Day--Fiction. 2. Brothers and sisters--Fiction.
3. Animals--Fiction.] I. Title.
PZ7.R88525Th 1999
[E]--dc21 98-51339
CIP
AC

Contents

1. Pumpkin Pie or Cookies?

Thanksgiving was
Harry's favorite holiday.
At Thanksgiving
you eat turkey,
cranberry sauce, and pumpkin pie.
Harry loved all three things.
"I love Thanksgiving, too,"
said Emily.
"I love turkey.
I love cranberry sauce.
But I hate pumpkin pie,"
she said.

"I can still love Thanksgiving
without pumpkin pie.
I can eat cookies
shaped like pumpkins."

Harry's mother was making
Thanksgiving plans.
She was making turkey plans.
She was making cranberry-sauce
plans and pumpkin-pie plans.
She was also making
cookies-shaped-like-pumpkins plans.
"Thanksgiving is not just
about food," said Harry's mother.

"What is Thanksgiving about?"
asked Emily.
"Thanksgiving is about
giving thanks," said their mother.
"Giving thanks for what?"
asked Harry.
"For turkey," said Emily.

"Thanksgiving is about giving thanks
for all our food," said their mother.
"When the pilgrims came to this land,
they didn't have stores.
They could not buy food.
American Indians helped them
to grow corn and other crops.
They showed them
how to make popcorn.
The pilgrims hunted wild turkeys.
They picked fruits and berries.
When there was enough food,
they all had a feast.

"The pilgrims wanted to give thanks

for all the good food.

That was the first Thanksgiving."

"We are not pilgrims,"

said Emily sadly.

"So we can't have Thanksgiving."

"Anyone can have Thanksgiving,"

said their mother.

"We can show how happy we are

to have such good food."

"Except pumpkin pie," said Emily.

2. No Nuts!

A squirrel ran across the yard.

It was looking for nuts.

It dug a hole in the ground.

No nuts.

"That squirrel forgot where
she hid her nuts," said Harry.

"She has no food," said Emily.

"She cannot have Thanksgiving,"
she said. "Poor squirrel."

A bird flew past.

It was looking for seeds.

The bird feeder was empty.

"That bird can't have Thanksgiving,"

said Emily. "Poor bird."

A chipmunk hopped over a rock.

It poked its nose into a hole.

It was looking for something to eat.

"She can't have Thanksgiving,

either," said Emily. "Poor chipmunk."

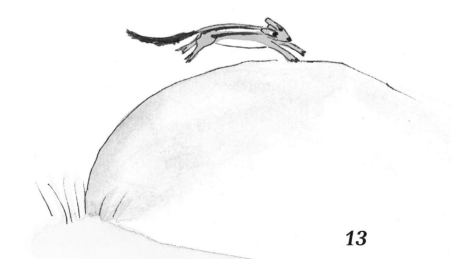

Harry and Emily

watched the animals.

"They don't have stores," said Harry.

"They are like pilgrims," he said.

"Let's help them," said Emily.

"Let's be like the American Indians."

"We'll have a

Thanksgiving beast feast,"

said Harry.

3. Beast Feast Plans

Harry and Emily made plans.

They made beast feast plans.

They made a list of animals.

They put squirrels on the list.

They put birds on the list.

They put chipmunks on the list.

Then they made another list.

Squirrels like nuts.

They put peanuts on the list.

Birds like seeds.

They put pumpkin seeds on the list.

Chipmunks like berries.

They put cranberries on the list.

Emily asked her father,

"Do squirrels like pumpkin pie?"

"No," he answered.

"Do birds like pumpkin pie?"

"No," he said.

"Do chipmunks like pumpkin pie?"

"No," he said.

"Nobody likes pumpkin pie,"
said Emily.

"Nobody likes it but Harry."

4. The Best Thanksgiving

It was Thanksgiving morning.

Harry and Emily's mother was busy.

She was cooking, boiling,

and baking.

She was baking lots of cookies

shaped like pumpkins.

Their father was busy.

He was cleaning the house.

He was setting the table.

He put out extra chairs for

Grandma Louise and Grandpa Joe.

Harry and Emily were busy, too.

They cracked peanut shells

and put the nuts in a bowl.

"These are for the squirrels,"

said Harry.

Emily found pine cones.

She and Harry put peanut butter

on the cones with spoons.

They rolled the sticky cones

in pumpkin seeds.

"These are for the birds,"

said Harry.

They took some cranberries.

They washed them with the hose.

They put them on a tray.

"These are for the chipmunks,"

said Harry.

Harry put strings
around the pine cones
and tied them to a tree.
Emily helped with the knots.
"Happy Thanksgiving!"
they shouted to the birds.
Emily put the peanuts
next to the tree.
"Happy Thanksgiving, squirrels!"
she shouted.
Harry put the cranberries
on the wall.
"Happy Thanksgiving, chipmunks!"
he shouted.
Then they ran back into the house
for their own Thanksgiving feast.

During dessert, Grandma Louise
looked at Harry and Emily.
"You two have been wiggling
in your seats all day," she said.
"Don't you like Thanksgiving?"

"We love it,"
said Harry and Emily together.
"Then why can't you sit still?"
Grandma Louise asked.

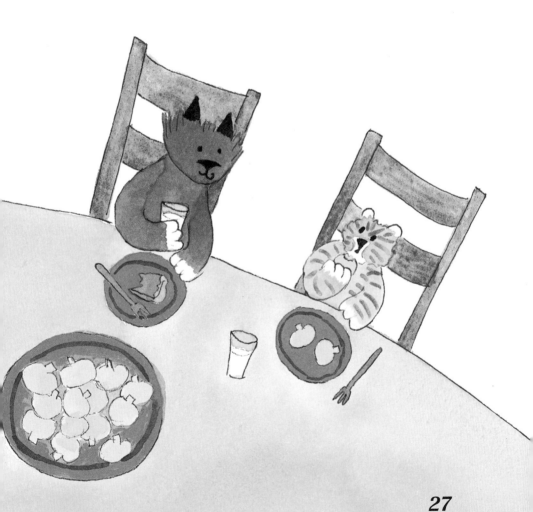

"We want to see if

the animals ate," said Harry.

He ran to the window.

"Look!" he shouted.

Everyone ran to the window, too.

"Oh, my!" said Grandma Louise.

Squirrels were eating peanuts.

Birds were eating pumpkin seeds.

Chipmunks were stuffing

cranberries into their cheeks.

"We forgot their dessert!"

said Emily.

She picked up a handful of cookies.

Everyone followed her outside.

"What a wonderful

Thanksgiving beast feast,"

said their mother and father.

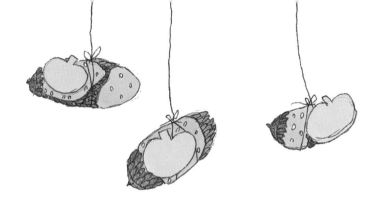

Grandma Louise smiled.

Grandpa Joe laughed.

They put some cookies

in the bowl under the tree.

They put some

on the sticky pine cones.

They put some on the tray

on the stone wall.

Then they all went back in.

They put the rest of the cookies
on their own plates.
They ate every single one.
"This is the best Thanksgiving ever,"
said Harry.